The Antichrist and the Artificial Intelligence (A.I)

(The Apocalypse according to Joshua)

by Juan Vitaliano Quiñónez Albán

This book is dedicated to all those who have felt a Revelation from God.

Seek and You will Find

CONTENT

$$93 = 9 + 3$$
$$9 + 3 = 12$$
$$12 = 1 + 2$$
$$1 + 2 = 3$$
$$3 = 3, 6, 9$$

ACKNOWLEDGEMENTS

To YAHWEH, my God, my Lord.

To Mr. Eduardo Delatorre, his wife and children.

To my friend and compadre Dr. Fabricio Barroso, M.D. who showed interest on my books.

To Joshua Torres, my friend, who had the courage to share this story with me.

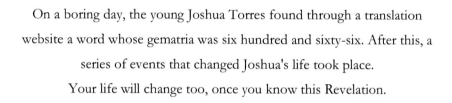

On a boring day, the young Joshua Torres found through a translation website a word whose gematria was six hundred and sixty-six. After this, a series of events that changed Joshua's life took place.
Your life will change too, once you know this Revelation.

1. INTRODUCTION

Before I start with this story, I would like to put you in context.

My name is Joshua Torres and I am Catholic, practicing and believing. In different parts of my life I have felt that I was in close contact with God, well, that is how I have perceived it.

I've always been someone with few friends, I'm not the popular one, neither the athlete. I am a geek of these times; however I have always felt that I am destined for more.

Now, at the age of 27, already married and with two daughters, through this story that I share with my friend Juan Quiñónez, I would like to tell you about my experience; a revelation that I had at one point, and about which I hope you can believe it; since it is the word of an honest man, and I do not seek to profit in any way from what is said here.

It is important that what I will relate below, rather than being fully accepted, should be debated, discussed, but not absolutely rejected. It is better to taste the bitter drink of the truth than to live a lifetime surrounded by lies. Lies, which will not only die with me (in old age I hope) but will also continuing, being manifested in my daughters, in their sons and from generation to generation if a radical change is not promoted.

The negative thing here is that the lies which I am refering to will not only be with me and my family. If somehow you (Dear Reader) are a believer, they will go after you, to your children, to their children, and will continue from one generation to another.

Perhaps Dear Reader, you are an agnostic, or an atheist, and if so, I kindly ask you to stay and read my story. As I do not expect conversion from you, the world will continue whether you believe or not in God; but the forces that belong to the world are those that must be revealed, as they operate in the shadows; they are silent like the snakes, and they hide as the rats do. And these are the forces that hold back the progress of man, regardless of our beliefs, our religion or a lack of these.

Let us begin…

2. THE ANTICHRIST

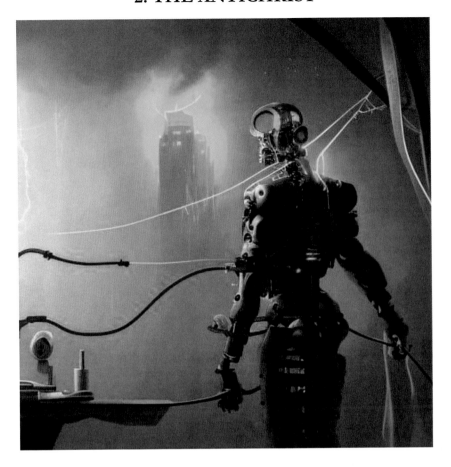

I was doing my homework that day. I felt as I was automated writing on my computer, but being also efficient and distant at the same time.

A movie came to my mind, that one called THE OMEN, where a child had a mark on his head; a mark which was the number of the beast.

- How can someone have a birthmark that is a number?

So I went looking on the internet.

The Internet was the best way I had for looking to answers.

And somehow, if the question I was asking was not well structured, then the answer was difficult to find; leaving more doubts than solutions.

Something went through my mind at that moment:

- What if numbers could be transformed into letters?

- What if 666 was a number that has a coded word?

Noticing this, I sent a WhatsApp message to Virginia. She used to self-described her as an Esoteric Girl.

Virginia, a friend and classmate from my high-school, was raised by her father. Her mother had migrated to Spain when Virginia was barely three years old, and they had little or no contact, apart from a few calls near Christmas or New Year's Eve.

Virginia and I, we weren't very close, in fact, if someone didn't socialize in high-school it was her. Although, she did have a group of friends (some hers and other of her cousins who she lived with). They used to get together on weekends to go partying.

Despite this, and since she described herself as "Esoteric", we frequently talked about various experiences I had during my last three years of school.

I told Virginia one day that we should discover what was beyond the "that number".

Nodding, she indicated that she knew something, since her father was of the Rosicrucian Order. And that within her knowledge, what she could tell me was that: not only was 666 the number, but other researchers said that it could be 616 as well.

I searched again in my web brower.

Per each answer the web browser popped me 10 more questions.

And I was able to see a video in my search, indeed, Virginia was right and that number could also be 616.

The documentary I saw mentioned that these two numbers (666 and 616) were a reference to Nero Caesar (ancient Roman Emperor) and that the reckoning for this analogy was through gematria.

I proceeded to look for another web page where I could calculate the gematria.

And after finding a gematria page, I searched on W-pedia for the name of Nero Caesar in Hebrew.

With the name Nero Caesar copied onto my clipboard, I put it into the online gematria calculator, and it gave me "that number".

What was stated in the documentary I saw was true indeed.

I was a Catholic back then, well actually always have been (and still am), so I said to myself:

- What if based on the Tetragrammaton of the name of God I obtain four letters in Hebrew that give me that number?

I found the following <<combination>> (scheme):

Shim = 300
Samej= 60
Vav = 6

Shim + Shim + Samej + Vav = "that number"

I put those 4 Hebrew characters into the web translator, and made a translation from Hebrew to Latin.

The translation gave me the phrase:

Y shhh!

Shhh??? (I wondered in amazement)

This doesn't have any sense, I thought.

I am going to change the order of the Hebrew letters (by changing the order of the letters, their gematria -that is, its numerical value- does not change) and I will obtain another word when translating.

I changed the order and this word appeared:

SHUSH

- What shush? (I told myself)

The word does not make sense:

Shush

That is similar to the gesture of silence (in Spanish*: Shhh!** Shu!).

* In English is the verb: To Shush.

** English.stackexchange.com:
ISBN: 9789100580360
(Fredrik Lindström's "Jordens smartaste ord")
discusses the word "shh" in depth and posits it's
perharps the only word common to most of the human languages.
It's even present in those languages that don't use the sound.

-It [Shush] does not refer to any person (I thought).

I changed the order of the Hebrew letters more times, keeping the translation from Hebrew to Latin, and suddenly...

The name LUCIUS appeared.

Lucius! Just like that video game's name?

Or Lucius, as Draco Malfoy's dad?

What does this have to do with the Antichrist?

Well, maybe Lucius from the video game is related to the Antichrist, but what about Lucius from Harry Potter?

What famous person from the time of the Roman Empire was called Lucius? (I asked myself)

Investigating, I came across Lucius Seneca.

Was he a poet, or am I mistaken? *

* Philosopher

Could Lucius Seneca have persecuted the Christian Church?

When suddenly in front of me a **"Revelation"** appeared

Lucius Seneca was the teacher of **Lucius Domitius Ahenobarbus** (grandson) better known as NERO CAESAR.

At that time I said:

What!

Was Lucius the name of Nero Caesar before he was emperor?*

* Indeed it was

Well, it makes sense (I told myself).

So I wrote to Virginia a couple of hours later.

- Look what I found (I told her).

I proceeded to explain what I found, and she told me: Interesting, but, what does it mean? You know that online translations have errors.

- Yes, DROSS* talked about that, well, more about the fact that these translations could give strange messages sometimes and he said that in a Top (7)

*DROSS: Famous Venezuelan Youtuber that lives in Argentina

It was at that moment that I decided to investigate if this Lucius and 666-thing was a mere coincidence, an error in the algorithm, or some bug in the artificial intelligence of the web translator.

That decision was **my point of no return...**

3. LUCIUS

A.I: An evilish kid named Lucius

who identifies

himself as The AntiChrist is staring at the camera

Well up to that point, I had found my 4 Hebrew letter combination.

Shim (300) + Samej (60) + Shim (300) + Vav (6) was equal to "that number"

So i said:

- I don't know Hebrew; maybe the Web-Browser is wrong.

Tomorrow I go to the QUESTIONS and ANSWERS app (QUO...A) and I will ask an expert why that 4 lettered Hebrew word was translated as Lucius.

Oh, by the way hehe, the 4 lettered Hebrew word is this:

In the QUESTIONS and ANSWERS app (QU...RA) on that day I found a Rabbi and I kindly request him through a post to tell me what the meaning of that word was, and if it was Hebrew or Aramaic.

The Rabbi answered me:

Shoshes (the 4 lettered Hebrew word), mmm I don't know it. It somehow resembles to the word for the **Shushan Purim** *holiday, but I don't see any sense or significance in the word SHOSHES.*

Perhaps it is some acronym used with the initial letters of someone's names. This is common in usernames on the internet.

- Okay, thanks (I replied).

But deep down, this whole situation seemed strange to me.

So I did not mention anything about it, at least for that day...

As I was asleep one night, I dreamed that a bearded man with black hair and about 45 years of age was teaching a class.

The man looked like Judas from one of those Jesus movies that are always shown on TV at the Holy Week *.

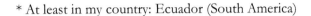

* At least in my country: Ecuador (South America)

This guy, in my dream, and dressed in an outfit like one of Jesus' movies told the class:

- PETER IS FOR JESUS WHAT JUDAS IS FOR THE ANTI...

He paused and did not finish the sentence. Apparently he was waiting for his students to finish what he was talking about.

We who were in the class didn't answer anything, but in my mind I understood that he was referring to the devil.

In my dream I said something like:

WTF??? (what the f… you know, hehe)

After that I heard a voice that said to me:

- What have I done to you Joshua? Why are you chasing me?

Suddenly in my dream I see people running, I am in a marathon. And, the person who was in front of me pulls out a knife and tries to kill whoever is in front of him at that moment.

Seeing that, I stop and suddenly some kind of Lucius Malfoy appears before me.

And he told me:

- All of this is the fault of the Judge of Just Cause...

And he looks at me mockingly, seeing me amazed and puzzled, and says:

- It is the Anathemism

At that moment I woke up, I did not understand anything about what happened, however I felt that perhaps I touched the sensitivity of some being of "lower astral" type (creature of the underworld or "low astral" – bajo astral in Spanish). So, I decided to talk to another people about my pseudo-discovery. Silence was my enemy here.

Perhaps Goo(gle)'s mistranslation…wasn't entirely a mistranslation.

I told myself then:

- This must mean something; it can't be nothing (worthless).

I must create some content, a blog post, or a video, where I explain how the word Lucius appears from the translation of the 4 lettered Hebrew word (pronounce as Shoshes)

So, I decided to make a video and I shared it via ONED…IVE with Virginia. In that video I explained:

1. That by gematria the order of the Hebrew letters can be changed. And the result of the sum of each of the Hebrew letters will remain the same.

2. That the word pronounced as Shoshes had a gematria of 666.

3. That Shoshes translated from Hebrew to Latin according to Google Translate was: Lucius.

I confess that when I was making the video, I felt that I had found one of the greatest discoveries in the history of the Catholic Church.

I had a high ego, and in my imagination I already saw myself meeting with the Pope in the Vatican, being awarded and everything else.

"It's so nice to dream..."*

* In Spanish: "Es tan bonito
eso de sonar"
Phrase of a song of the
Spanish song-writer Alejandro Sanz

In the end Virginia received my video, I think that due to her tasks and other occupations she did not see it, despite the fact that she swore to me that she had seen it completely.

Unlike Virginia, whose mother migrated to Spain, my mother, who was a single mother, came from a wealthy family, had about 4 franchised pharmacies, and despite this (I understand that for safety too), she urged me to take the bus and avoid at all costs the taxis (even worse the pirate taxis*), since in my city**, they kidnapped people a lot in these units.

* pirate taxi: Not a yellow cab.

This type of taxis are

when a random person

(not corporated or affiliated to a taxi company),

decides to drive and carry passengers

as yellow cabs do. Similar to an Uber Driver.

** In Guayaquil (Ecuador-South America)

was common that many people was kidnapped or assaulted

by the so called "pirate taxis", but sometimes the corporated taxis

or afiiliated yellow cabs, used to commit crimes as well

What I'm trying to say is that unlike Virginia I had more free time (to spend watching videos and "playing" with online translation sites).

As an interesting fact, the video I posted (the one I sent to Virginia) had **more dislikes** than likes, and not only that, it made that many of the few subscribers I had (on my music channel) (I forgot to tell you that I'm an amateur musician), well, most of them unfollowed me of my YOUTUBE channel.

4. VIRGINIA TAKES DISTANCE FROM ESOTERICISM

IMAGE GENERATED THROUGH ARTIFICIAL INTELLIGENCE (A.I.)

Virginia had the characteristic of not letting go of the phone from her hands, even during classes. She was the type of person my mother tends to classify as a "cellphone-glued hand person"[*].

* Cellphone-glued hand person:
A person who eats with the phone next to him/her,
handles the phone the whole time during classes,
goes even to the bathroom with the cellphone.
Spanish: Pasa pegada (fem.) al teléfono.

One day Virginia and I were leaving school, and she told me:

-   Let's go downtown*, I'm bored.

* Downtown of Guayaquil city (Ecuador-South America)

Downtown was a place where Virginia liked to go, but I personally found it uncomfortable and unsafe, but I went with her anyway.

-   Let's go - I told her, and we stayed walking (window shopping*) until we got 8 at night.

* window shopping in Spanish:
Mirandear o Vitrinear (going to a store
to watch and buying nothing)

Suddenly she asks me:

Josh, do you remember Steve Huff?

- Yes, of course, the Youtuber who talks to the dead.

Yes, him. Look, I downloaded an app that was recommended on his channel, it's called Echovox, and is said that it allows you to talk to the dead, is it okay if we use it?

- Mmm, okay, but I'm suspicious of that thing, we better not ask anything when using it, let's just press the play button and let it run.

Okay, but hold on until we get to the Metrovía's* bus stop, there are a lot of thieves around here (she said).

> * Metrovía: mass public
> transport system in Guayaquil (Ecuador)
> that have buses stop with a ceiling,
> a guard and you pay a fee for the entrance.

You know, "parcero"* (that's how she called her friends and she wasn't Colombian) my grandmother was a Medium (Psychic).

> * word used in Colombia
> for "friend" (informal use)

- Which? The one on your mother's side or on your father's side?

My daddy's mom (says)

- Oh okay, and where was she from?

From France, but my father and I have zero French skills, "parce"*; just our surnames. (She said)

> * Parce: abbreviation of parcero
> (Colombian word) for friend
> (Informal use)

We arrived at the Metrovía bus stop. Virginia lent me her earphone, turned on the Echovox and we listened simultaneously.

The Echovox started echoing all the ambient sounds near us and the app interspersed them with a bank of random words or phonemes pre-recorded in the app.

Suddenly from the Echovox this started to sound...

Josh

Josh

Josh

Josh

I immediately took off my earphone, I was full of fear.

A cold feeling invaded my body; the Echovox had said my name.

Suddenly the Metrovía arrived, Virginia said goodbye and I was really intrigued, especially since I couldn't chat with her during all my way home.

My brother was asleep at home, I felt uncomfortable in the silence of the night, so I decided not to eat. My mother had gone out a few minutes ago with some friends and left 4-year-old James lying down and tucked in. She didn't call me, I only found a Post-it* on the refrigerator door, in which she told me that she would be late that Thursday's night.

*Post-it notes

I went to my brother's bedroom frequently to see how he was. I was worried if he was breathing properly. He was just a kid, and mom wasn't a devoted mother. So, I assumed that competence because of her.

I touched James's forehead, he had fever. He stared at me and said:

- Josh, I can't sleep.

I didn't say anything to him, and then I tried to turn off the light in the next room. This was the one that barely illuminated James's room. Suddendly as I turned it off for a second, little James told me:

- Do not turn off the light...

That's how time passed and was 2 in the morning. At intervals I approached James and place a damp cloth on his forehead, in order to see if I could lower his fever.

My mother did not answer the cell phone and since it was late, I knew that she could not bring any paracetamol syrup from a pharmacy, since there was none at home, and I felt distrustful of ordering medicnes through delivery service due some news of assaults that were committed by delivery guys during those days*

(Yeah, you might remember that I mentioned that my mother was the owner of some pharmacies but an old phrase says: *shoemaker's son always goes barefoot*).

* In Ecuador you can buy most of medicines without a Physician's prescription. There is also allowed to order prescription medicines (without a Physician prescription) through home delivery (directly from the Pharmacy or through delivery apps like Glovo (until 2020))

I was angry with James that night, since the next day I had classes and he didn't let me sleep, so, when I saw him apparently asleep, I proceeded to turn off the light and then I laid down on my bed that was in the opposite room from his.

Only 10 seconds have passed since I laid down and I heard James running and screaming desperately towards me.

His scream sounded demonic, sort of like a possessed kid from movies.

James throws himself towards me and with only four years old he raises my head, while I am face down, and suddenly he turns my head sharply as if he wanted to kill me by turning it, all this, without ceasing to scream.

(Just like horror movies)

- James, you son of a bitch!!!! Get back to sleep for fucks' sake!!!! (I yelled at him)

James, stopped yelling, and ran to his room with a funny stride, (similar to the Chucky doll) and then he lay down on his bed quietly.

It was around three in the morning and James had less fever.

My mother hadn't arrived yet, so I proceeded to send Virginia a WhatsApp message:

- You won't believe what happened to me (sorry for writing you so late)

Surprisingly, Virginia read my message and then I told her what happened.

After that I went to the sofa in the living room, because that whole James thing made me uncomfortable. And to tell the truth, I didn't want to be next to him.

Virginia answered me and just said something like:

- You are living the phases of a horror movie xD xD

I read her reply and fell asleep.

It was 4:30 in the morning, I realized that my mother had already arrived, but when I was on the sofa in my living room, everything was relatively dark, afar I saw a dim light, I couldn't move at all; I only could see what was in front of me.

I was lying on my back on the couch, staring at the floor, unable to move.

I wanted to move and I couldn't.

I was through some kind of sleep paralysis.

Suddenly I heard leather boots approaching to the sofa where I was.

I saw someone dressed in black leather coat and black leather boots, but I could not move.

It was then that I felt a weight like a hand on each of my shoulders.

Suddenly I realized, and for my own surprise, that I was dreaming.

I couldn't sleep for the rest of the morning, and I was all stressed out. I was supposed to be in class at 8 a.m.

I realized that this time I "hit a nerve" of some entity or "low vibrational demon". And worst of all, that the problem of this entity was not only with me, but like a mafia, it had manipulated my younger brother to try to attack me.

"If the Mafia can not hurt you, they will hurt someone who you love"

They hurt me, not in body, but in my soul; as I saw such a small and playful child acting that way; As if he was possessed by the devil himself.

Later at breakfast, my mother was kinda mad for her last meeting, James was happy and shining. Fever was gone and James did not remember anything that happened. On the other hand, I felt like shit.

At High School, Virginia had not arrived. She used to have the habit of constantly drinking with her closest friends.

Please exclude me from this group, as I was not her close friend and only talked with her about paranormal phenomena.

It is so, that I assumed that she had not gone to class since she had a hangover*.

* In Ecuador the hangover is called "chuchaqui"
(Pronounced as choo-chah-kee)

The weekend went by and Monday comes. On that day I talked to Virginia and she told me:

- Parce*, the morning that you wrote me I was having insomnia, while the following Friday night I went to a bar with some friends.

* Abbreviation of "Parcero", Colombian word for Friend

I wanted to go to the bathroom in that bar and there were two girls in the row before me.

As soon as I got close to the row, the first girl walked into the bathroom and lingered. I couldn't see her face.

The other girl, the one that was in front of me, seeing the delay of the first girl called the guard in order to check what was going on.

The guard knocked on the door - Virginia told me in amazement-. But no one came out, so the guard went to get the copy of the keys and proceeded to enter the bathroom.

Once entering, no one was in the bathroom, the girl in front of me was scared and we both looked crazy because the guard thought we were drunk.

- ¡Loco!* (Virginia told me).

* Loco means "dude"☺ (Informal)
During a conversation
this word is not related to mental diseases (crazy).

I prefer not to get involved into any esoteric thing; I think I've reached my limit.

Josh, if you're going to talk to me, talk to me about anything, but please avoid talking of paranormal issues.

- Well (I told her), - Take it as a coincidence, maybe you saw something that was not real-

Here at this point in the story, Dear Reader was when I was left alone in my search for truths and little by little Virginia got distanced from me…

5. THE ROSICRUCIAN GENTLEMAN

Done through A.I: THE ORDEN OF THE ROSEN CROSS

Now with Virginia distant from paranormal subject, my curiosity about Lucius and my search in the Goo... Translator still continued.

On one hand I had failed as a Youtuber. My discovery that the word Shoshes translated from Hebrew into Latin was Lucius, have not been properly taken by my Catholic brothers on the internet.

- What Antichrist? - They tell me

- Antichrist, are all those who are against the Roman Catholic Church!

- Haven't you heard about Hitler? He was an antichrist!

In a certain way, Hitler was a disastrous character for society, but he does not differ much from other world leaders, be they Chinese, Russian, North American or British, who to their credit have the same number (even higher in certain cases) of victims in their respective genocides.

But, on the other hand, I investigated, and, to be Antichrist, there were two basic conditions, which the world has not yet seen.

1. A temple in Jerusalem is required (but, it is difficult there, since there is a mosque where the 2nd Temple was).

2. The Antichrist must enter the temple of Jerusalem and exalt himself above God, saying that he (the antichrist) is the true God.

And obviously, this "prophecy" is not fulfilled by any of the infamous genocidals to whom I have alluded in previous paragraphs.

I think that my Catholic brothers (by indoctrination of the Catholic Church) are confusing the term: anti-Christian, with the character The Antichrist.

The Hebrew-speaking community of Quo... (The APP of QUESTIONS and ANSWERS), had not given much attention to my query, apart from the answer that a Rabbi kindly provided, regarding Shoshan Purim as an analogy of my tetragrammaton (an infamous tetragrammaton btw).

Similar to Virginia's attitude, I had put these issues aside (so called paranormal issues), and quite rightly I hadn't had used the Echovox either.

My other friends were also suspicious of what I had found. And when many of these whom I will identify as "ALELUYOS*", saw my posts on my social networks, they not only removed their subscriptions from my networks, but they also told me:

* ALELUYOS: (plural) religious phanatics, similar

to Holy Rollers

- Seek help with Father Antonio (the high-school Chaplain)

- You need God's help, talk to Father Antonio, look for Father Antonio.

What for? (I replied myself). So that he explains to me the theory of the antichrist, which is everyone who is against the Roman Catholic Church?

So with Virginia distant and with my other friends ignoring me every time I told them about this topic, my curiosity grew bigger.

I was at my computer one afternoon and I thought:

- If the Rabbi told me that Shoshes could be associated with Shushan Purim, then I am going to do a research about this holiday.

Shushan Purim commemorates the blockade by Esther and Mordecai to a plan of the Vizier Haman (Persia), who wanted the destruction of the Hebrews who lived in the city of Susa, occurring on the 14th day of Adar (approximately equivalent to the month of February in our calendar). However, thanks to Esther, the Persian King Ahasuerus allowed the Jews to defend themselves against this attack, and they were victors. This according to Esther's account.

It is so, that I do not see much relationship between the word Shoshes and Shushan Purim, but nevertheless, I, in my linguistic cocktail (everything is mixed up), decided (arbitrarily) that Shoshes (Lucius according to the translator) could be a variant of the word Shoshana meaning: rose.

As a fact of interest: on Shushan Purim, the Hebrew people were compared to a rose when reciting the Shoshanat Yaakov (or Yaakov's (Jacob) rose) prayer on this festivity.

Under this criterion I found the following analogy:

Shoshana (rose) = Shoshes (word translated as Lucius according to the G... Translate).

I found that Shoshana or Shushan not only referred to a rose, but could also refer to a flower (i.e. a lily)

A lily for example could even be a reference to an Egyptian lotus.

I found that according to the author Karl Josias Von Bunsen (if I am not mistakenly writing his name) lilies or lotuses in ancient Egypt used to be called **Sesen**.

Sesen was coincidentally the name given to the god Sos, Sôsis.

Sôsis was another name of the god SHÛ.

Sesen was another name for the city of Hermopolis, or literally the Polis (city) of the god Hermes, i.e.:

Sesen as object:
- It is a lotus, lily, rose or any flower

Sesen as a city:
- It is another name of the city of Hermopolis.

Sesen as a deity:
- It was another name of the god SHÛ, Sos, Sôsis

According to the ancient historian Manetho; Sos, Sôsis, Sesen, was another name for the Egyptian god Thoth.

And Thoth is how the ancient Egyptians knew Hermes (Greek deity).

I will emphasize that:

Sesen as deity = Sos, Sôsis, Shû, Thoth, Hermes.

Sesen as an object: Lotus, flower, rose.

Sesen as a city: Hermopolis (city of Hermes also called Sesennu).

Sesen according to Josias Von Bunsen also meant: THE EIGHTH.

"THE EIGHTH", a term that "coincidentally" appears in this phrase from the book of Revelation:

"The beast that was, and is not, is himself also **THE EIGHTH**, and is of the seven, and is going to perdition".

Revelation 17:11

New King James Version

All these associations I decided I had to share with someone, but with Virginia distant from me; who would be interested in this!

- "Father Antonio will hear you" (would say some religious fanatics at my High School), although he, if he found out about my investigation, would more than certainly order me to be expelled or sent to a psychologist, and that because the Inquisition no longer exist.

I proceeded to write all this that I am telling you on my laptop, and in one of those days Virginia approached at the end of a class and told me:

- Joshua, sorry to bother you, but, my boyfriend is going to be busy today, and during this time I've been staying with my father and stepmother, instead of my cousins in the apartment. Do you think you can accompany me to see my suitcase? It's that Mizael (her boyfriend) is working and I'm afraid of being robbed.

Okay, after school we're leaving (I told her), is that okay with you?

- Yeah, sure.

Until Virginia was ready, I proceeded to go to an Internet Café* and luckily I had a flash drive with my research on it, so I printed it out. There were like 10 pages.

* Internet Café:
Cyber Café in Ecuador:
A place where you rent computers
for searching on the internet
but there is NO coffee (it is only a name Lol)

After that, I waited for her outside the school.

With my research ready, Virginia and I took a taxi (from a taxi company that the students of our High School used to take).

Near her father's house we were about 1 hour from where she lived and 2 hours from where I lived.

While we were in the taxi I told her:

- "V" (that's how I used to call her), do you think I can give an investigation that I printed to your dad?

I know that he is from the Rosicrucian Order and all that stuff, and since these topics kinda make you cringe, well, I would like to see if he is interested.

Okay (she told), "él es chévere"* (she said)

* Él es chévere: "He is cool" (in English)

Already in the house of Virginia's father, her father came down to open the door for us, he was of advanced age. Entering his home I could see on one of the walls of the garage that the image of the eye of Horus was painted (it could have been the Eye of Ra too I don't remember).

I asked Virginia when I saw that representation:

- And what does that mean?

Mmm I don't know (she told me), things that my father comes up with.

We went up to the second floor, I assume they rented the first one, I don't know this.

And once on the upper floor I sit at the table and the man sits next to me while Virginia went to see the suitcase, and then I say to him:

Sir, Virginia told me that you are interested in antiquity topics (I didn't want to tell him that I knew he was of the Rosicrucian Order).

So, if you don't mind, I'd like to give you this.

(I proceed to give him the brochure I printed).

And Virginia's father kindly asked me: What is this?

I replied: It is a **Biblical investigation** that I have done.

And Virginia's father looked at me with an uncomfortable face, as if he was disgusted by my brochure.

- Hmm... Nah, I don't like the biblical stuff. Keep that bible away from me (He told me while laughing).

Well hmm... (I told him) it's more about apocalyptic themes and numerology, cultural and deity comparisons between ancient civilizations.

Hmm okay (Virginia's father told me intrigued), it sounds interesting... I'm going to read it.

Only 3 minutes passed, and Virginia already had her suitcase ready, I said goodbye to the "Rosicrucian Gentleman" and we went with Virginia to wait for a taxi.

After that, already in the car, I told Virginia to please remind her dad to read the text I wrote.

Virginia agreed. After that we talked during the journey, I got close to her house (since her home was a place that only her closest friends visited) and in order not to spend on a taxi I got off, and decided to walk, it took me three hours until I arrived home ☺.

A few time later our High School years were over and we (Virginia and I) lost contact, except for two or three times that we chatted over the years.

In the last chats, she told me that she "had found the Lord Jesus Christ" and that she was now an Evangelical-Christian.

Good for her! I thought, since once (and despite everything she lived through) she told me that she did not believe in God and that perhaps we ourselves were our own God (yes, Dear Reader, sounds like blasphemy, but I respect it)

I never knew if the Rosicrucian Gentleman read my text or not...

I preferred to assume that he did read it.

Two years later I translated the word from Hebrew into Latin again:

In the new translation the name **Lucius did not appear.**

Now, appeared the word: SHUSHAS

A word that I later associated with the ancient city of SUSA.

I don't know if you remember what I mentioned in previous paragraphs about this city:

> Shushan Purim commemorates the blockade by Esther and Mordecai to a plan of the Vizier Haman (Persia), who wanted the destruction of the Hebrews who lived in the city of Susa, occurring on the 14th day of Adar (approximately equivalent to the month of February in our calendar). However, thanks to Esther, the Persian King Ahasuerus allowed the Jews to defend themselves against this attack, and they were victors. This according to Esther's account.

As an interesting fact, one of the most important deities of SUSA, according to Sumerian records, was the goddess Inanna, who was called by the Babylonians as Ishtar.

6. DREAM OF A NIGHT OF HELL

Drawn by Artificial Intelligence: Dream of a night of hell

Bianca was my impossible love.

She was the woman that every man in school wanted to have.

Since this is a linear story, I will get out of the sequence.

And was Bianca the first person who had to pay for my thirst of curiosity.

Rashelle (pronounced Rashél, but we called her Raquel) Virginia's friend, had made a comment that she found me attractive, and Virginia, who had a matchmaker reputation, proceeded to introduce me to her.

I went out on a date with Rashelle, she was a fan, like Virginia, of going to the Guayaquil's downtown; she liked seeing clothes and not buying. The curious and novel thing about this was that Rachelle invited me. So I assumed that she was interested in me.

On a second date, Rashelle appeared with Bianca, the "unattainable woman" from High School, who was Rachelle's best friend. I had to go "window-shopping" with both (thus damaging my plans with Rashelle I thought), however, and as we had a great time I realized that Bianca was a nice person, a virtuous woman and a pure soul.

Days later I went out with Rashelle alone again, and while on the Metrovía, I tried to kiss her, and she coquettishly avoided my mouth. She told me to stop that cuz we were nothing more than friends and that she "couldn't do that to Bianca". And I obviously surprised, without understanding anything, told her:

- And Bianca, what does she have to do with you and me?

- Bianca likes you (she told me), and the truth is, I like you too, but I am interested in a boy, and we (Rashelle and that guy) have been knowing each other for a few months, so if you haven't noticed that Bianca likes you, then

I advise you to do something quickly, or another guy will be her boyfriend first instead of you.

Surprised by what Rashelle had told me, I decided one day to ask Bianca out, and we went to a discotheque (yes, being underage hahaha, we won't be the first or the only ones)

At the disco Bianca told me:

- Josh, I'm surprised you asked me out. Look, I don't want to make Rashelle mad.

No, everything is cool, she's just a friend, in fact she mentioned that she has a guy she's interested in, so you don't have to feel bad or anything haha.

- Rashelle, she hasn't told you anything about me, has she?

No, not at all (I lied her)

Long story short, I will only say that it was a magical night, Bianca ended up being my (official) girlfriend from that very night (first time that has happened to me haha lol)

The next day, and as people became aware of it, no one could believe what was happening.

The quiet one in the classroom (I'm not a fan of AK-47s just in case xD), managed to pick up the unattainable girl from High School, who was not only extremely beautiful and intelligent, but was also a unique woman in every way.

On the other hand, Rashelle, started a relation with the boy she was interested in but they lasted 12 days and they never spoke to each other again haha. #Nohate, Rashelle.

A few months later, with Bianca as my girlfriend, I had told her all the "paranormal" adventures that I lived with my friend Virginia. Being Bianca, a devout Catholic, she told me that everything I have told her seemed interesting, but she considers that there are certain phenomena which it is better not to know, and that there are things, especially those of an evil source, that should not be studied; Because studying it means worshipping the devil, and it is better not to give him any type of relevance.

This is why, despite loving Bianca deeply, even up to now (and I think it will be for life), I have never made her participate in any of my researchs.

Not only because of the way she thinks, because of her faith, but also, because of the following story that I will tell you:

One day I was randomly and meaninglessly adding numbers on a calculator, as if to see if I could find anything.

Suddenly an idea came to my mind:

What if I take from the book of Revelations all the numbers related to God, and I put them in one column and in another column I put all the numbers related to the devil, and then I add each column independently?

Indeed, I did so, do not ask me quantities.

After having both columns filled, and with the results of the addition, I proceeded to divide the amounts by each other (I don't remember if the good numbers were divided by the bad ones or vice versa).

The result of that operation was:

$$36,6180339887$$

Yes, it might seem strange to you how I know the result, and not the quantities that I used to obtain it. And the reason is that I wrote the result, but the sum operation I threw it away.

36.6180339887, I rounded it up to 37.

After that I started to add the number 37 by itself.

$37 + 37 = 74$

$74 + 37 = 111$

$111 + 37 = 148$

$148 + 37 = 185$

$185 + 37 = 222$

222 + (37 * 3 or 111) = 333

333 + (37 * 3 or 111) = 444

444 + 111 = 555

555 + 111 = 666

What a strange analogy! (I thought)

What do 37 have to do with 666?

And how did I get to 37 after doing a calculation with the numbers from the book of Revelation?

One day doing an investigation I found the term:

Sacred Geometry

And then, I search on Google the term:

Sacred Geometry 37/73

After that I searched for the definition of a "Star Number"

"A star number is a centered figurative number, a centered hexagram (six-pointed star), such as the Star of David, or the board on which Chinese checkers are played."

Taken from Wikip…

The first 13 star numbers are 1, 13, 37, 73, 121, 181, 253, 337, 433, 541, 661, 793, 937.

These numbers are represented by the following image:

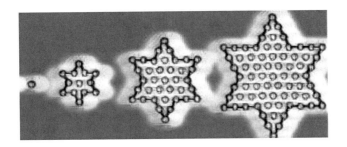

If you count each ball (from the first image: left to right)

- The first is the number one (1) (has one ball)

- The second is the number thirteen (13) (has 13 balls)

- The third is the number thirty-seven (37) (has 37 balls)

And through this search I found also a drawing related to the number 37/73 (a.k.a. 37 is the palindrome of 73) (yeah, like Sheldon Cooper mentioned in the Big Bang Theory, lol)

So, one day I printed the 37/73 star, and I forgot that sheet at Bianca's house.

The sheet has this image on one side:

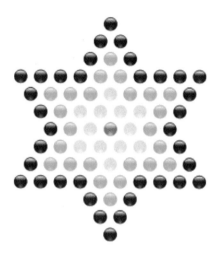

37/73

And this Facebook image on the other side:

Visual Representations of Doubling Sequence of the number 37

Bianca saw that figure and she thought that it was some sort of random image or a senseless design, so she kept it next to her bed, in order to giving it back to me once she sees me again.

The next day Bianca sent me a Whatsapp message and she told me that a nightmare she had around 5 a.m in the morning, in which she had dreamed the following:

Bianca was in a desert and in the distance a woman's voice was heard saying:

Nero

Nero

Where are you Nero?

After that, Bianca saw a woman in black who looked more like a demon and said:

Do you know why He hates the pig?

Bianca, could not move or respond, and this being tells her:

[He] punished him for his sins, and therefore his head is of a pig's.

Bianca proceeded to see a guy with a pig's head, the pig was rotten, and a lot of flies were landing on this head.

- "It's because of his pig's head," (the woman told Bianca), that this being is known as the **Lord of the Flies.**

After that Bianca continued in the desert and listened:

Nero

Nero

Nero

Lucius

Lucius

Lucius

Come, I won't hurt you; It's me Lilith, your friend.

Bianca then in her dream saw me lying on my bed sleeping.

And this woman says to Bianca while pointing at me:

- Look at him. He is not good, He is mine.

And Bianca told her:

No, no, he is good, and he is from God, and I love him.

After that Bianca heard the woman say:

NOOOOOOOOOOOOOOOOOOOOOOOO

Drawn by Artficial Intelligence: Lilith the demon

Bianca woke up very scared.

She told me that the dream seemed so real.

Despite the fact that Bianca was a highly educated woman, and due to her religious background, I was able to notice several strange themes as a result of her dream:

1. Bianca knew of the Emperor Nero but she was unaware of his association with the Antichrist.

2. Bianca didn't know the demon named Lilith.

3. Bianca did not have a good memory for these paranormal subjects, so the reference to Lucius (the Google mistranslation), or to the video game of the antichrist boy named Lucius, well it was a horrible and dark reference in her dream.

I deduced that everything could be a coincidence, so I didn't take it too seriously, and on the other hand, I was looking for my hexagrams, which I had lost, but I didn't know that Bianca had it.

On the next day Bianca wrote me again, and she told me what happened a few hours before at 7 in the morning when she was still sleeping.

I dreamt that I was in a humble apartment (Bianca told me).

And suddenly I listened to my 5-year-old niece calling me in the distance.

When I got closer to where her voice came from (since I couldn't see her), I heard her saying with an adult voice:

Bianca, help me please! (with anguish and despair)

Suddenly I woke up, and I got up from my bed in a hurry shouting:

Mari, Mari, my love

And while I was screaming, I advanced into the living room (I was completely awake in here), and Mari and Pancho (her two nephews) were there.

They looked at me scared, seeing me scream.

Bianca pauses.

It is the first time that a dream is so real and I have been having horrible nightmares for two days in a row.

- I only told her: Pray, and do the sign of the cross.

Already changing the subject, Bianca told me:

- You left a strange piece of paper, with a drawing. What is that?

Oh! You have it hehe, that's a number pattern, don't mind it haha (I tried to hide that I was nervous).

Can you give it back to me?

- Yes, I have it here, Bianca told me.

She had slept next to that paper those days.

When Bianca told me that I was really nervous.

The forces of evil have not only went after my brother James, like that time that I used the Echovox, but they had also been after Bianca, after I found that interesting pattern with the number 37.

Apparently the evil forces don't like you printing hexagrams.

By the way, as an interesting fact: Emperor Nero Caesar was born in the year 37 CE

I had to be careful not to let Bianca see my research. And so it was.

Months later I told her that perhaps what happened was about that hexagram that I printed.

And she remarked:

Josh, stop caring about to those issues, perhaps it is "The Evil One" who wants you to exalt him.

I told her:

- No, because I am a man of faith, and if there is someone who wants me to speak without fear, that someone is God. Yahweh, my Lord.

7. SESEN (THE 9TH GATE)

If the Ishtar Gate was the Eighth Gate of Babylon

The SESEN gate is the 9th gate

Drawn by Artificial Intelligence: The Sesen Gate. The ninth gate of Babylon

Years had passed and I already had a university degree in Process Engineering and I was working in a food factory.

I married my beloved Bianca, with whom we have two beautiful girls; my brother James is also doing well and just this year, he is about to finish school, and well, my mother, she, was still the same haha.

One day at work, the areas were being radically cleaned, and I had finished filling out the documentation for the manufactured lots. At that time, and to be honest, I felt tired and didn't want to go home, apart from that it was hard to get a taxi, and there were no company buses available, so I stayed for a while doing nothing at the factory.

Suddenly, I remembered the phrase from the time I dreamt of that Lucius Malfoy cosplay in my youth, and the phrase echoed in my mind:

"This is all because of the Judge of the Just Cause (insert a mocking smile in here from that guy with an excess of knowledge while my face is pale of ignorance)... *it is the Anathemism"*

This word: Anathemism was unknown to me.

I entered the online search engine at my workplace, and found a book on chaos magic (I barely know what is this), and this book identified Anatheism with self-destruction.

In other words, the Lucius Malfoy cosplay was telling me that "self-destruction" (anathemism) was fault of the Just Judge of Cause (maybe a possible reference to Father God).

I understood then that perhaps it was The Antichrist who manifested himself to me (or he might be an emissary).

Which seemed somehow ridiculous to me: What do I have, above the fathers of the Church? How can I arouse the interest of this being?

It seemed more like a suggestion (an idea of my mind), so I let it go.

Another day, and with the work on my part already completed, the theme of the Sesen (the lotus, the lily, the rose, shushan, shoshanna, shoshan) came to my mind.

I asked myself then:

What Middle Eastern deity would be associated with the lily, the sesen, or the lotus?

So I found that the lily was a symbol used by the goddess Ishtar (of Babylon).

Ishtar was the Babylonian version of the Akkadian/Sumerian goddess: Inanna.

Inanna could be dual (male and female) and under this characteristic she was called Ninsiana (this word was another name by which the planet Venus was called).

I later found within a web search the article by Dr. Martin Schwartz who is a scholar in Near Eastern Studies (Orientalist).

Dr. Martin had an Academic Paper in which he had mentioned a lost deity called Sesen (yes, like the lotus), a deity anciently revered in present-day Iran and also revered in the Aramaic pantheon.

I looked for Dr. Martin on the Internet, I found his email, and I wrote him, asking if the relationship between Sesen (Egyptian) and Sesen (Aramaic) was that both represented the same deity, and, before this Dr. Martin completely denied my statement. He even seemed annoyed about what I said hehe.

Weeks later coincidentally my email was hacked, my emails got deleted, and I had to reset my user.

Despite this, I deduced that Sesen (Egyptian) who represented Eshmun (Phoenician god, I had not commented on this before), Sos, Sôsis, Hermes, Thoth was the same as Sesen (from the ancient Aramaic-Iranian pantheon).

Sesen (representing the lily, lotus) is the symbol that linked the Egyptian god Sesen with the Babylonian deity Ishtar (equivalent to Innana (deity called Ninsiana, a word that represented the planet Venus)).

Venus, who is the name of a Roman goddess, was also known as **Lucifer.**

SESEN = THOTH = HERMES = INANNA (Ishtar) = Venus = Lucifer.

That is to say that the famous Shoshes (from my Tetragrammaton) is the one and only, the infamous **LUCIFER.**

8. THE DREAM OF A REVELATION

It happened during my annual vacation that I experienced long periods of sleep. I assumed that it was due to the fatigue due to rotating schedules.

My daughters were with my mother-in-law, and I tried to spare my time writing down as much as I could a series of dreams that I had.

And I will call this part of the work:

THE APOCALYPSE ACCORDING TO YEHO

THE APOCALYPSE
ACCORDING TO YEHO

Apocalypse. - From Latin Apocalypsis, and this from Ancient Greek ἀποκάλυψις (apocalypse = "revelation")

To Reveal = make (previously unknown or secret information) known to others.

To Reveal = To Unveil

THE APOCALYPSE ACCORDING TO YEHO
(CHAPTER I)

1. While I was asleep, a man's voice came to my mind, resounding with a strong echo. I am Yehó, he exclaimed, and I come to you with a message from the Most High.

2. Because there are many faces that masks and costumes use. But in the end the truth prevails over any illusion.

3. And it is that between heaven and earth there is nothing hidden, and in the end every veil must be revealed.

There is no word that is eternal, unless it comes directly from The Creator.

Write then what I leave in word.

Listen to the proclamations of YEHO

ABOUT LUCIFER

Of the stars

The Sun

4. Lucifer is a dual being and is related to the stars. The sun, venus, the earth, the moon, and jupiter are the representations of him, and to these, tribute should not be paid, even worse veneration.

5. Because if the stars shine it is due to The Most High, and if we attribute them an own life, it is nothing more than a device of the False Light Giver.

6. Because the sun is light and life in nature, only by the work of the Most High; being so, do not conjure the sun, do not pray to it, and do not exalt it. Flee from its cult and avoid the tabula solis or magic square of the sun at all cost.

This tabula solis is an invocation of fallen angels. The sum of their numbers is an affront to The Creator.

So avoid adding their numbers [of the tabula solis], do not draw them, and do not reckon them.

There is only one true number, and it is the number of The Eternal. It is the number that comes only from the word of God.

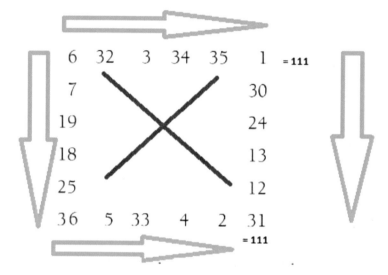

7. Do not design or arrange altars, temples or atriums as instruments of veneration of the sun.

Do not build structures that play with the sun's rays. And it is that the Infamous through his spirit can write using the sun.

8. Do not use the Sol Invictus* [Invincible Sun] in your temples, instruments of worship, and do not make any reference to it in your religious art.

[Search in Google: Sun invictus Christianity]

Leave the stars to poets, philosophers, and learned people. It is the Most High, the Invisible One, to whom the stars must worship. Man should not pay reverence to the sun.

Venus

9. Venus is a representation of the Infamous one. He was never an angel; He has always been a usurper. Lucifer was a traitor to his parents. Let this being distanced from God. Be him Anathema.

10. If stars and planets draw figures in their movements, these come from the work of the Lord.

Do not draw or represent the movements of the celestial bodies, so avoid the pentagram of Venus and any other enemy of God.

Of Venus and its pentagram you will not make any design or construction.

Keep Venus and her pentagram away from temples and places of worship and prayer.

Do not design or draw the flower of Venus, whether it is alone, or associated.

Because in the false flower of life is the hexad and the number 6 (SSS -of the Brotherhood of the Serpent-) of the Infamous Usurper. A sign of The Deceiver.

11. With these beings removed from the grace of God there are no absolutes, since sometimes they seem to be opposite and different, other times they are the same body with different representation.

12. Of Aphrodite, Ishtar, Inanna, Ninsiana, Hecate, Diana, Demeter. Oh women! Do not take them as female models of struggle or morality, since they are dual beings, and they are nothing more than different costumes of the Infamous Usurper.

<u>Planet Earth</u>

13. Respect your planet and take care of its resources, but do not call the earth: Mother.

Mother Earth is just a representation [of the Infamous].

Mother Earth is an image of the mother goddess, and this is nothing more than an archetype of The Usurper.

But what comes from heaven is only from The Everlasting God, and there is nothing and no one before The Father Creator.

14. Many others are the stars and planets related to the slanderer.

However, I will not refer to these, since what I share with you is a message of life, and life comes only from God our Lord.

Jupiter

15. Do not worship the Io-Pater, do not venerate him.

The one who calls himself Jupiter or Zeus is just a disguise of the same archetype and is nothing more than an infiltration.

16. And it is that wise men and linguists, what I am sharing with you, they already knew; however they reneged on God.

Because the word day, dyeu-, Zeus, and bright sun were all terms created in their minds and between meetings and conspiracies, they only sought to generate usurpation.

However Zeus has been relegated, and is nothing more than a deity who will never reach the height of his letters to be called GOD.

And it is that the wise men and linguists motivated by the False Sun*. They transgressed the name of God.

* PARHELION DEUS

They wanted to associate Father God with Jupiter and they used to call HaShem as:

Iouæ, a fake god.

They changed the "u" for "v"

Iovæ

They kept playing with letters and vowels, losing all fear of God.

Changing the æ for the vowel "e" in that name.

They changed "I" for "J"

And this they did exalting themselves, and in mocking directly to the Wisdom of God.

They were corrupted by their egocentrism to pay homage to their false deity the JOVE FATHER (Iovæ) PATER; JOVIS-PATER, or false creator father.

JovisPiter

JuvisPiter

JuPiter

Are names of usurpation.

They sought to syncretize HaShem with Zeus, mocking and making fun of The Name of God.

But the time has come for a New Revelation to be known.

Since no one should make fun of others, much less of Our Lord.

That is why you have been chosen, because He Who Seeks Finds.

And in your mind you have the dream of a world where love reigns.

There cannot be a God in a Church, where there is lack of empathy. Where idolatry has been shown and that has not only be cause of conspiracies but also pain.

And it is that you Joshua, through what you write, will make the word known, of The One whom from now on the world will call: **YEHO**.

But woe to those who doubt without seeking!

Woe to those who want to refute just to exalt their wisdom!

Leave to The Creator what belongs to The Creator, and give to Science, what belongs to Science.

Those self-proclaimed as scholars and intellectuals will seek to refute thee.

But everything that is refuted must have evidence.

17. This is why The Infiltrator* has managed to be silent as a serpent in various religions.

* Greek: Ο διεισδυτής

For The Usurper there is no single cult. This one only seeks **UBIQUITY**.

That is why whoever reads this text must be brave.

As there is no worst fear than speaking the truth.

These Anathema beings like to be silent as Harpocrates.

And more than silence they exalt themselves spreading blindness, not of body, but a spiritual one.

There is no worse ignorance than that derived from not opening your eyes and clearing your mind.

There is no worse sin than silencing those who seek God's love to prevail over lies and evil.

The past influences of the Church Fathers often clouded their judgment and reasoning.

And this bias was taken advantage of by The Evil Disseminator.

Woe to those Wise Men, Scholars and Prophets!

Who drank from the vine of abomination!

They have exchanged the eternal for lust and sin.

They have been corrupted and are corrupting, all this in the absence of God.

Because they do not have God in their hearts or in their minds.

Only in their word, but there is not word without action.

They seek to punish the just and set the criminal free.

Joshua you will be seen, as a heretic and apostate of God.

That's why I ask you to be constant and brave.

Because there is no better criticism than the one that comes from who has been inside.

And it is better to be self-critical than to be questioned by those who do not know the Lord.

Having said this, which I have proclaimed, YEHO disappeared from my dream.

18. It is so, and up to here, that I, Joshua Torres, author of this book, testify to what I have seen, leaving it in writing, so that whoever wishes to search, may find it.

19. And if someone here wants to debate what has been said, then debate it, but beyond the dream, what has been said here is true. Nothing of what I have written can be denied or demolished, because what is revealed here definitely does not come from me, but from the Most High.

THE APOCALYPSE ACCORDING TO YEHO
(CHAPTER II)

I did not discuss with anyone what I saw and recounted in Chapter I.

However, I was intrigued.

I feel, as I write this, enormous pressure.

I deduce that it is evil who seeks to stop my publication, generating fear in my readers and fear in me.

That is why before telling you my second dream, I will pray and I hope that you, Dear Reader, will pray with me:

Oh Father God, have mercy on me.
Since I am a sinner.
Allow me, O Lord Jesus Christ, to have health and will
In order not to give up and be able to post
everything that has been manifested to me.
Do not allow, O Lord, that evil inflicts damage or disease on me.
Heal O Lord Jesus Christ, all my ills and diseases, whether they are known or unknown
to me.
Heal my spiritual illnesses
and you, O Lord Jesus, enter into me
so that through your divine mercy
calm down this sorrow that stalks my heart and that bothers my spirit.
With the glory of Father God
You who live and reign
forever and ever

Amen.

It is so that I will relate what my Lord YEHÓ revealed to me in a second dream, in order to be able to bear witness to His revelation.

HIS NAME IS YEHOH

1. The voice of YEHO appeared before me in a dream and said to me:

Write down the following, as I tell you, and without any pause. In case you don't understand something, continue copying.

(...) I [will] record the noble deeds of Jehosh'a, son of Nun, the successor of the prophet of God in whom be perfect peace: and the gifts of God to [unintelligible], and his help, and the victory over the enemy, and his triumph over the kings, and his slaughter, and how he took their lands, and their division among the nine and a half tribes: and I will mention some particulars

of what happened to him in the war with the kings, briefly, and compendiously, and by way of epitome, [incomprehensible] and [incomprehensible], if God, whose name is exalted, wishes. It is then said that Jehosh'a when he undertook the conquest of the country, and the war with the nations there, said to the princess of the people by God's command, after having made them promise that they would not join the worship of others to that of God, and that they would maintain the observance of the law and its statutes, they and their posterity after them until future times. Get up and tell the whole congregation to prepare everything necessary to enter the land of Can'anm that God, the God of your fathers, swore to give you. And they gathered the tribes, and brought them to him, and being in his presence, he said to them: Know that your God, he is the one who fights for you, he will destroy your enemies before you, and he will make you possess the land, the land that he swore to your fathers that he would give it to you as an inheritance: I testify to you that you remember God, and that he will not cease from your mouth, and you will prosper in all your works. And the people answered Jeshosh'a and said to him: We are in your presence submissive to your word, and as we obeyed Moses, so we will obey you; and anyone who opposes your command will be sentenced to death. And Jehosh'a sent two men to spy out Riha: and they went in and lodging with a woman named Ra'b, one [unintelligible]; and her house was by the (river bank). And the king heard about them, and sent the woman by night, and said to her: Bring out the men that came to you. And she hid the men from the king's messengers, and said: Two men of the messengers of Jehosh'a the son of Nun came to me, and they left immediately from the gate of the city before it was shut. And he went in pursuit. And the woman came to the messengers of Jehosh'a and said to them: "The king will certainly send men to locate and seize you, but I know in truth that God has delivered this city into his hands, and has put the fear of you in the hearts of its inhabitants: for indeed they have heard what happened to Phar'un and to the sons of Misr, and what God did to you in the Sea of Colzum, and of the manna that fell on you forty years, and of the defeat Amalek, Sihun and 'Og, kings of the Amorites; and the people of the world are afraid of you, therefore I want you to make a pact with me to treat me as I have treated you, and tell your lords what what has happened. And when God has delivered this city into your hands, you will save me and all my house from the slaughter." And they made a covenant with her on these terms and swore to her. She then made them go down with a rope from the top of the wall to outside the city, and she told them: Go to Mount Jabal so that no one finds you. And they set out and came to Jeshosh'a, and told him what had happened to them. And Jehosh'a gathered the people together, and said to them: Arise, advance, and pass over the [Ordonna?]; and do not fear, for God has given the earth into your hands. And he said to them by the word of God: "Know that the ark of the covenant of God passes before you, and there will be between you and the Imams who carry the ark of a thousand cubits, so that God can fulfill his work with you. And while Imams are crossing in the water, shout with a great mighty voice". And Jehosh'a immediately arose and entered [Ordonna?], and when the Imams bearing the ark crossed the waters, all the people cried out with one voice:

YEHOH our God is one, YEHOH.

YEHOH mighty in war

YEHOH is His name.

2. What I have told thee is my union with past times.

And something else I tell thee: Beyond the name, what matters is compliance of the Law.

ANTICHRISTIAN SIGNS AND SYMBOLS

3. Various are the symbols associated with the enemies of Christ.

4. There are various signs associated with the spirits of the stars, and these beings are enemies of Christ.

The Rose

5. The Rose as a symbol of secrecy or hermeticism should be avoided in temples and places of prayer or worship to God.

If there is any decoration with roses, these should be away from images of Saints.

The rose like Shushan (shoshanna) represents Isis.

The rose of Isis is a representation of the space pentagram of the planet Venus.

The word "Mystic" should be avoided in names of saints that have the word rose.

Roses are hermetic, symbols of Hermes and by Isis through association.

Beyond symbolizing love, or some detail of friendship, there should not be any analogy of the roses with the names of the Saints.

The lotus flower and the lily

6. Delete all reference to the lotus flower and the lily of Christian faith.

7. The lotus whose name is Sesen and the lily, whose name may be Shoshan, are symbols of Isis and Ishtar. And both are the same!

The Evil One expresses himself through these objects to exert his infiltration.

Scholars of the Law of God are advised to purify any association with the lotus and the lily, especially in Saints through whom no reference must be done to the Rose, the Lily or the Lotus or Fleur de Lis.

The Harpocratic Gesture

8. Harpocrates, youthful representation of Horus, who is called by the wicked as False Christ, to whom occult circles attribute being born in December and having risen from the dead as a means of confusion and infiltration of the Evil One, through his false messiah: The Antichrist.

Eliminate all reference to the Harpocratic Gesture of arts in temples and cults; as well as their texts.

Harpocrates is also the son of Isis

9. Erase from the Church of Christ any analogy to Isis and Harpocrates.

10. Sesen, the ancient Iranian deity, is nothing more that an infiltrator in the Church, and shall be eliminated.

The starting point for this purification is Saint Sisinios of Partia and Saint Sisinios of Antioch. Both, infiltrations of the False Light in the Church. Symbols of the Infamous known better as: **THE HOLY RIDER**.

The fallen angels **Senoy, Sansenoy and Semangelof**, are another archetype of Sesen (Lucifer) and they are only a merely infiltration of SESEN in JUDAISM.

These fallen angels are nothing more than an archetype of Lucifer through the description or story of a conflict between Sesen (Lucifer) versus HaSatan and the demon Lilith.

TALKING WITH THE DEAD

11. Listen O People, the proclamations of YEHOH!

Listen to Him and you will be saved.

Ignore him and you will follow a difficult path of the Kingdom that will Come.

12. Listen O People!

Stay away from new forms of communication with the dead.

Let the dead rest in peace.

For those who have been righteous and God fearing are awaiting judgment.

Refrain from using modern means to write to the dead.

Do not use automatic writing, spiritualism or shamanism.

The summoned dead cannot reason, and impure beings eager to enter the real world can be found with them.

Refrain from using modern means to talk to the dead.

Stay away from portal-type media*.

(* ITC = Instrumental Trans Communication)

RESTRICT ARTIFICIAL INTELLIGENCE

13. Great is the ambition of the human being.

And in his ambition he puts both mind and hands to work inadequately.

Wisdom is a gift from God.

The intelligence of man is of divine's will.

Do not put intelligence at the service of machines.

Do not put the machines at the service of mankind.

Because those worshipers of the False Sun are the ones who intend to exalt machines above man, thus exalting themselves...

(My Lord Yehoh proceeded to keep silent)

After that, he gave me a message that I couldn't hear...

And I woke up.

ASSIMILATING THE DREAMED

If from the bases (even if they are ideological) everything is wrong, it is obvious that the body of the Roman Catholic Church (applying also to its resulting schisms and sects), well everything is going to be wrong.

What is required for a renewal?

My Lord YEHOH never told me to move away from my faith.

He was punctual in that everything, what he told me in my dreams, should be published.

Could it be that a second coming of the Messiah implies a fundamental reform in the Roman Catholic Church (and why not the Orthodox)? (The true -Messiah- not the false one who will seek to rebuild the temple of Israel and sit on his throne)

Definitely and analyzing, I am only a man of faith, but beyond being a scribe or copyist, or dreamer, well, I am nothing more. I am not a Theologian, a religious leader, or a religious scholar.

A reform in the Church obviously requires a strike force, with the logistics and the courage to take the reins and put down so many years of symbolism and infiltrations of The Usurper in our faith.

How would the Muslim brothers take this situation if it happened in the future?

Why did my Lord YEHOH refer to the Biblical Joshua as Jehosh'a and not name him to me as Yehoshuah or simply Joshua?

Why did my Lord YEHOH in his story not mention the city of Jericho as Jericho but rather told me that the city was named Riha (Ríhá -another name for Jericho-)?

Why did my Lord YEHOH, mention the Imams (name used for Sunni Muslim religious leaders) and not refer to them as priests?

If I were the one chosen by YEHOH, what would I need to start a reformation (both in the Roman Catholic Church and in all the patriarchates of the Orthodox Church)?

I assume that I alone, I will not be able to do anything.

I did not comment to anyone on what my Lord YEHOH revealed to me; I simply decided to publish it online, since if The Infiltrator is on the networks, then a bit of truth or rather, an unmasking in his own territory would be suitable.

I hope that up to now, everything I have revealed is of your interest.

My name is Joshua Torres, and I think that God revealed himself to me in **all His majesty.**

That is all I have to say about this matter

I hope Dear Reader, with permission of The Most High, we meet again.

Best Regards.,

Joshua Torres

SUPPLEMENTUM AD HUNC LIBRUM

JOSHUA FIGHTS AGAINST THE BEAST OF ARTIFICIAL INTELLIGENCE

I was with my cell phone one night watching TikTok.

And curiously, the TikTok algorithm was making me esoteric and paranormal recommendations beyond the usual: Jacobo Grinberg, Madame Blavatsky, Chris White from Bible Prophecy Talk and similar topics.

I already had the impression days ago that the Tik Tok algorithm could read my thoughts.

Topics began to appear, which I had not searched for in years, and even worse, some videos found were about situations or theories that I had thought about for a while, but that I never dared to look for. That is, I thought about it and it appeared to me on said network.

YOU THINK IT, THE ARTIFICIAL INTELLIGENCE GIVES IT

I was alone at home on that occasion; neither my wife nor my daughters were with me, they had gone out for a walk with their grandmother.

YEHOH appeared before me briefly in a dream while I was on that social network.

I just heard YEHOH say a name that sounded like Gerard Massy*

*Gerald Massey

I felt that He wanted me to read more and research this author.

I was looking for <<G. Massy>> on the internet when suddenly a vision appears in front of me when I was almost falling sleep.

I could see several small robots, and little by little these were grouping together.

The sound like hammering steel that came from a machine was clear; it seemed to be that a bigger machine was assembling itself in front of me.

I could see an apparition of a humanoid shaped machine.

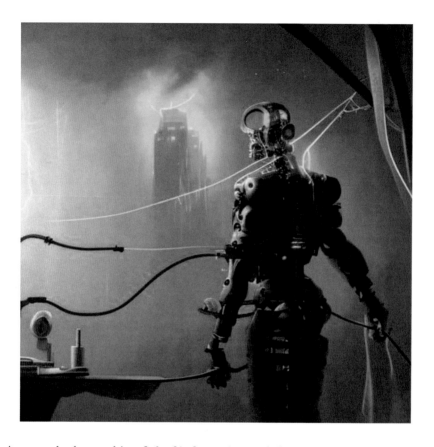

Apparently the machine fed of information and the cameras next to it were some sort of an eye, through which it can see everything (THE ALL SEEING EYE or the eye of Ra).

I saw behind me several people dressed in white, but I couldn't see my body.

Just like Joshua once did, people were screaming the name of YEHOH and we were rushing into a battle with Artificial Intelligence.

Before starting the fight, I woke up…

The message was clear.

The False Light is on the internet.

It is developing.

It is feeding.

It is waiting for the right moment to attack.

But God, who is always one step ahead, will not let evil win.

Whether if The Beast is in a human form, as the text of a book, in some ritual or inside the internet.

YEHOH will defeat ARTIFICIAL INTELLIGENCE...

THANK YOU FOR READING

Juan Vitaliano Quiñonez Albán

Email me at: EDLT PUBLICATIONS

publicationsandcompany@gmail.com

ABOUT THE AUTHOR

Juan Vitaliano Quiñónez Albán, a "fiction" novelist, brings us his second book in this genre, after his work **"WISDOM OF THE ANCIENT SECRETS (FROM THE PERSPECTIVE OF A CHRISTIAN)"**.

THE ANTICHRIST AND ARTIFICIAL INTELLIGENCE (The Apocalypse According to Joshua) is a fantasy work with reference to the book: **Samaritan Chronicle of the Book of Joshua**, fused with real Christian eschatological findings, shared by Joshua Torres during the use of web applications in his adolescence and adulthood.

THE ANTICHRIST AND ARTIFICIAL INTELLIGENCE (THE APOCALYPSE ACCORDING TO JOSHUA) shows us a story in a current scenario in which the devil (Lucifer) manifests himself through artificial intelligence on the internet and behind translation pages, blogs and social networks.

It is a work that geeks who are fans of mythology, esotericism, Christian eschatology and why not religion will enjoy.

Made in the USA
Columbia, SC
26 January 2023

75187449R00060